CW00482104

Belinda Blinked; "Lockdown 69"

A very special Belinda Blinked for very unspecial times;

By Rocky Flintstone;

Artwork by Mouldy Wood;

Chapters;

The delivery van moved off slowly. 24 single beds lay stacked in the Steeles head office carpark.

'Hrrrrmmph...' fumed Sir James, 'a fine kettle of fish this is.'

'Now now, don't get excited Jamsie…..' exhaled a fraught Countess Zara, 'think of my pet chow a wow locked in my St Petersburg flat… it doesn't bear thinking about.' She sniffed.

Belinda looked anxiously out of her office window; it had a glorious view of the Steeles car park and enabled her to monitor all comings and goings. It reminded her of the widows watch she had at the top of her house in the Bahamas. She hoped the mattresses would be comfortable, divan sprung would be just the ticket. That thought prompted her to look at her watch, where was he, it had been a simple task and one that she'd entrusted to her top RSM. At that moment an old dirty yellow coloured panel van coughed and spluttered it's way to the office entrance. The driver jumped out, looked up at Belinda's office window and put his thumbs up... he'd got them!

Quietly and without a fuss, Des Martin started to unload his packages…… they were small and light, something anyone his size could easily handle. Each parcel bounced as it hit the ground…. a sign of the Gods perhaps, but alas it was natures way, tightly bound toilet rolls always behaved in that fashion.

Belinda exhaled a heavy cloud of tension released CO2....

'Thank God,' she thought, 'at least we can all excrete in decency.... and they'll be very useful in mopping up any excess fluids that might escape from.......'

Her mind was jolted from it's thought pattern as her senior Special Account Manager charged into her office.

'Belinda....... I want to go home.... I mean it's not an unusual request, I've got 3 weeks holiday owing and I want to take them....... now....'

Bella settled herself on the mahogany desk and let her naked cervix expand over its polished surface. Her readily flowing juices trickled across the desk and Belinda thought of toilet roll, mopping them up, swishing them down.... but thought again....... fuck it......... lets do it the old fashioned way.

After Belinda's pep talk, Bella understood that she had to play the game.

"Lockdown 69" was for the best... a team effort, something to work at and show true effort, it would be hard... but the benefits could be amazing...... a new job... promotion... the world was her oyster. Promotion to Head Person Australia was on the cards. Bella's little tootsies curled up at the prospect.

Belinda's office phone rang urgently.... three times. On the third ring Belinda answered,

'Blumenthal here...... what's up?'

'Hi Belinda, Tony.... get your fat arse up here now and bring Bella...... we've got some screwing to do, and she needs the experience.'

Tony put the phone down abruptly..... a sign he was under pressure.

Belinda gasped……. 'she needs the experience…' not the Bella Ridley she knew.

As they walked into Tony's outer office, Maeve looked up and smiled her wonderful Irish smile,

'He's got you both some presents…' she breathed out deeply.

Bella and Belinda turned away instantly… garlic breath was for vampires, not senior sales execs.

'Not your average Irish meal,' Bella squeaked at Belinda, 'should be cabbage pie, or even toads in potato…. my fav… will the canteen be serving it?'

'Not on my watch Miss Bella.' Belinda replied harshly. She too was becoming fraught, Tony's telephone manner had her on edge and she didn't mind admitting it… that was of course if anyone asked her.

Tony shouted through to Maeve, 'Send them in pronto Maeve, otherwise we'll be here all night!'

'On you go,' Maeve replied softly, 'and the best o'luck to youse.' She smiled sweetly and Belinda thought of demotion letters. This employee was getting ahead of herself.

The two girls walked through the doorway and immediately four silver objects flashed through the air bound directly at their tits…

Belinda reacted immediately and with Ninja like reactions caught two of the flying objects cleanly in her hands. Bella wasn't so fast, but her natural assets came to her aid as the two items each hit a large boobie and fell to the ground safely.

'Wow Tony…… didn't know you were such an expert shot.' exploded Belinda.

Bella just grunted and rubbed her mammaries gently, eventually letting go a soft expletive.

'Ffffffffffuuuuuuuuuuuuuuuuccccccccckkkkkkkkkkkkkkkkkkkkkkk…'

'Years of service in the army, just telling you that for background info.' said Tony.

Belinda nodded and looked at the objects in her hand, one was a box cutter and the other a screwdriver. Bella's was the same.

'Why these Tony and more pertinently, why us?'

'Goes with the territory Belinda, sales people get the shit jobs… and believe you me, this is a shit job.' Tony sighed remorsefully.

'We could resign!' shouted Bella still rubbing her titties.

'Is that a request or a statement?' Tony asked with a menacing look clouding over his facial features.

Belinda replied harshly now starting to lose it too.

'Let's not be hasty Tony…. let good people go and they'll never come back… and I ain't hiring some dumbos just to fill shoes when all this is over…'

'Sorry Bella… yeah you're right Belinda… let's stick with the trash we already have, God help us….'

Belinda sighed, Bella burped…. lunch had been very satisfactory.

'Ok,' Tony continued, 'sit down and let's do this.'

Bella and Belinda grappled for the one soft luxurious brown leather seat normally occupied by Maeve when she was taking dictation.

'Ah, ah, ah…. Bella, seniority rules and seeing as I'm the Sales Director, sorry, International Sales Director and your boss, I'm pulling rank. Sorry…'

Bella let go of the chair suddenly and Belinda stumbled with it on top of her into the office wall.

'Ok then Boss,' Bella replied sweetly, 'I'll just have to do with this hard, straight back plastic thing someone somewhere calls a chair.'

Bella sat down suddenly hoping she'd crush it into the ground and get ten sick days leave. Perhaps a nice insurance claim for whiplash… that'd be a bonus.

The chair buckled, it's plastic legs straining under the wake of the unsuspected attack….

At the very last moment the resilience of modern day plastics came to her aid and the chair held its structure.

Tony shook his head, now he'd seen it all.

'First question Belinda…. where's Jim Thompson, I need an update on sales numbers.

'Good question Tony,' Belinda replied nonchalantly whilst Bella looked at the ceiling and started whistling. 'he's on honeymoon.'

'Honeymoon!' Tony scoffed, 'what do you mean honeymoon… the guy must be all of 58 years old!'

'Maybe a late starter?' interjected Bella.

'No he's not Bella, Peggie Strumpethouse is his fourth wife, you know her, the one with rotten breath in purchase ledger.'

Bella answered too quickly….

'That cow… she knocked back my new leather swivel chair two months ago.'

Tony interjected feeling things were getting out of control again,

'Pray tell me dearest Belinda just where are they honeymooning?

'That's the problem Tony, they're stuck in some South Sea Island, they can't get back…'

'South Sea Island, South Sea Island! Belinda, we're paying these people far too much…. a South Sea Island… I ask you!'

Tony sorted a sheaf of papers on his desk and asked his next question.

'So Belinda, tell me has the entertainment… sorry slip of the tongue, the training lady arrived yet?'

'Natasha Biles….? Yes they're in reception with Paddy the Barman getting key cards organised.'

'They!' shouted Tony, 'you mean there's two of them?'

'Yes.'

Tony put his hands in his head and screamed,

'Fuck, fuck, fuck, fuck… is she Welsh too?'

Belinda answered,

'With a name like Samantha Jones I would think so boyo…'

Bella looked at Belinda and mouthed,

'He's losing it….'

Belinda Blinked;

Tony calmed down, just a little, Maeve popped in with a cup of steaming hot coffee and offered Belinda and Bella a Gin and Tonic.

'Ohh yesss please, slurp slurp...' replied a sucking in air Bella.

Belinda smiled and nodded thinking, 'Perhaps I've been a bit harsh with Maeve.'

Tony sipped his coffee and continued,

'Those tools are your next priority, you saw the 24 beds delivered to the car park, well they need unpacking and assembling... I did warn you it was a shit job.'

Belinda nodded, this was something she could delegate to her team. She'd love to see Bella and Ken Dewsbury assembling a single bed... there'd be legs and tits everywhere. Feeling so much better with this thought floating around in her head Belinda smiled and said.

'Absolutely Tony, consider it done.... Anything else?'

'Yes, as a matter of fact, and this is very delicate, so keep the info to yourselves,' he glowered at Bella, 'if possible...'

Bella hicced a little and answered,

'Absolutely Boss, absolutely.' and knocked back the rest of her drink.

'One bed per office, excepting the conference room, Sir James has claimed that... two beds, bolted together... he likes his comfort.'

'You mean Countess Zara likes her comfort.' added Bella bitterly.

'No, not so,' Belinda interjected, 'If I remember rightly, she's just as happy on a stage floor.'

Tony barged on; this meeting was taking up more time than he'd planned.

'Ahem, a further two beds... bolted together in here....'

Bella sniffed.

'Of course Tony.... only natural, Maeve's office is too small for any size of bed... totally understandable...' Belinda added naughtily.

'Yes, well, it is a nice big office, shame to not put it to good use.' Tony blushed.

'Now here's the sticky part.... we're putting the RSM's in the leather room.'

Belinda laughed loudly and long...... 'You're what???????? Tony have you really lost your marbles... they'll kill each other before the first day's over. Guaranteed!'

Bella sniggered........ 'You'd better remove that fancy drinks cabinet then.'

Tony looked at Bella and said,

'Good point Bella, I knew there was a reason I wanted you in this meeting.'

'I'll have another GnT then, my mind is so much more lucid when I've had some alcohol... Maeve?'

'So that's the accommodation sorted, now food. I've managed to strike up a deal with Harold's Emporium of Knightsbridge, purveyors of fine wines and foods.

We're doing a barter arrangement, our pots and pans for their groceries.... I think we'll come out better on the arrangement.'

He smiled and leaned back in his chair, pleased he'd negotiated such a good deal.

'Fine wines, Tony,' noted Bella... 'Chardonnays? Perchance?' she smiled and thought,

'Perhaps this lockdown isn't such a bad thing at all.... hic...'

'Nearly finished,' continued Tony, 'as you know there's a meeting of COCK at 5pm this evening and afterwards dinner at the Pentra. All of us are invited, it's only a two mile walk so Des Martin has agreed to take Sir James and Zara over in his van... they being elderly and all that. Your pal the Duchess has organised it.'

'The Duchess is here?' Belinda observed in a somewhat amazed tone.

'Yes, it's all hush hush I'm afraid while this flap is on, but she's asked me to tell you, you've got a meeting with her after dinner. She'll fill you in amongst other things then.'

Belinda grinned, there was only one sort of "filling in" the Duchess would need with Belinda.... never mind "amongst other things..." especially after an alcohol fuelled Pentra dinner.

Bella chimed in,

'I think I'll forget about my 4 inch heels tonight Belinda... two miles is a fucking long way... and there's no pubs to break the walk...'

'Tell you what Bella,' said Belinda kindly, 'we'll fill our freebie Jim Stirling thermos flasks with Chards before we set out. I'm sure we can find a friendly bench to sit on half way.'

Bella smiled and belched, Belinda always had the best ideas...

Back in Belinda's office she summoned her sales team. Des Martin, Ken Dewsbury, Patrick O'Hamlin, Dave Wilcox, and Bella Ridley. Maeve was "busy" with Tony so couldn't attend.

'Righto,' Belinda brightly addressed her troops.

'This is a job we need to get done in the next two hours, as we've all got a COCK meeting at 5.00pm sharp.'

A murmur of apprehension and excitement went around the RSM's. The last COCK meeting they'd attended had ended in a bomb explosion.

'Here are your tools.' Belinda handed each RSM one tool each.

'First, we get all the beds unpacked with these box cutters, then carried upstairs to the offices... one in each, keeping back 8 for specific roles which I'll explain later. Once they're in the offices we'll assemble them with the screwdrivers.... Pretty simple stuff, but critical to a good nights sleep. That's why we in sales have been tasked with this job... senior management know we won't fuck up.. alright! Let's go.

Belinda lead her team out into the carpark and pretty soon all the beds were sitting in a row ready for phase two of the operation. The packaging had been stuffed into Des's old van and everything was ship shape.

After a bit of huffing and puffing the sales team had manhandled the beds up to the first floor where the offices were. Soon each room had a fully assembled bed in it with eight left over as planned.

'Now,' said Belinda, 'put two into the conference room and screw them together.'

'Shall I put an official sign on the door, Boss, saying official bonking room? asked Des Martin.

'No Des…. you don't want to do that. Next two beds into Tony's office, again screwed together. Leave the remaining four out here.'

Dave Wilcox piped up,

'Boss, four beds… four RSM's… you're not putting us in this cold draughty corridor are you?'

'No Dave, we've got a much better place… what about the cold storage room next to the kitchens?'

Dave Wilcox blanched at the thought, whilst the other 3 RSM's laughed at Belinda's joke.

With only four beds remaining Belinda grabbed the nettle by it's throat and gave her last instructions.

'OK team, bring these to the Leather Room'

'The Leather Room,' Patrick O'Hamlin gasped, 'I always thought it was a myth… a company hearsay…'

Bella smiled and said, 'Yes, only the privileged get in there…. Isn't that so Belinda?'

Belinda continued unabated, the bit of leadership now firmly between her teeth.

'First remove the drinks cabinet to Tony's office… it cost a fortune and we don't want it bust up.'

The RSM's entered the Leather Room looking around in awe at the sheer comfort, never mind elegance of the leather décor. Carefully taking a corner each of the drinks cabinet they manhandled it down to Tony's office and plonked it in a corner.

'Now place the four beds towards the top of the room, we don't want to impede access to the secret meeting room.'

Belinda went over to the false wall and moved her hands. With a grinding of electronics the outside corridor merged with the Leather Room entrance leading down the ramp into the private meeting place where COCK gathered. It was so discrete, no one would ever guess the Leather Room existed, until now. But uncertain times called for uncertain measures and besides, the RSM's had to bonk somewhere.

Belinda Blinked;

Chapter 3

Dribble, Drabble and Babbel;

It was 4.45pm, Belinda slowly went back to her office with her mind now focused on the COCK meeting taking place at 5.00pm. It would be a tough meeting, the truth would certainly be exposed as to why they found themselves in such difficult circumstances. She would need to be strong for her team… and herself. But even she didn't know the full story, only Sir James had complete access to the bizarre situation. She swivelled around in her chair taking a last couple of minutes of quiet before entering the ring. A sudden movement outside caught her eye. A shiny dark brown Rolls Royce had just manoeuvred itself off the main road and into the Steeles Pots and Pans carpark. It regally glided to a halt in Sir James Godwin's private parking place.

Belinda breathed in quickly…. 'There'll be hell to pay if Godwin catches them there.'

A smartly dressed gent jumped out of the driver's seat and took off his chauffeur's cap, tossed it into the passenger seat and shut the door gently. He walked briskly to the back of the vehicle and opened the trunk. From it he extracted a small black briefcase, tucked it under his arm and locked the Roller. Seconds later he walked into the main reception of Steeles Pots and Pans.

The time was 4.57 precisely as Belinda picked up her notes and ran to the leather room, joining the other members of COCK queuing to enter. The RSM's stood to attention as she approached and Belinda smiled, glad not to hear any moaning about their sleeping places. Bang on 5.00pm Sir James appeared with the chap Belinda had spotted in the carpark in tow. He growled at Belinda,

'Come on woman, let's get this over and done with.' He unceremoniously grabbed Belinda by the left arm and took her with him into the secret meeting room.

'Hrrmph... better introduce you... Mr James Dribble, of Dribble, Drabble and Babbel Forensic Accountants, meet Belinda Blumenthal our International Sales Director.

Belinda and Dribble shook hands,

'Your reputation goes before you Ms Blumenthal.' Dribble said coolly.

'I wish I could say the same for you Mr Dribble.' Belinda replied.

'Ahh... that's the nature of my game Ms. Blumenthal, working in the shadows of numbers... but some of my acquaintances have told me you're no slouch in the shadows game yourself.'

Belinda said nothing and sat down beside Sir James. Mr Dribble sat next to her and opened his black leather briefcase. Belinda glanced at it and thought she should get one just like it.

The large video screen burst into life and amidst a lot of crackling the image of the Duchess appeared. Everyone except Jim Stirling was present and silence took over the room. The shiny glass table reflected the sombre mood of the Knights as Belinda stood up and started her introductions.

'Welcome everyone and you too M'aam.' as she pointed at the screen. The Duchess nodded her head and calmly adjusted her tits, but remained silent.

Belinda continued,

'We've assembled you all here as we unfortunately have some major news to impart about our company Steeles Pots and Pans. With that said

I'm handing over to Sir James Godwin who has the up to date situation on his finger tips. Sir James.'

'Hrrmmph, thank you Ms Blumenthal, I shan't beat about the bush like I normally do, but quite frankly we've been robbed. All our cash and bank accounts have been cleaned out and what with everything else, I'm afraid we're down to our last tin tacks. Any questions?'

Bill from HR stood up and said, 'How, Sir James?'

'Frankly William, we don't know, four days ago everything was normal, but since then we've had all our credit lines cut off. As you know the car leasing company has taken back all our vehicles this morning, no one will supply raw materials to the factory...'

Ken Dewsbury interrupted Sir James,

'Sorry Sir James, but is there any possibility of getting our natural effects back from the cars... I left two furry dice hanging from my rear view mirror...'

Dave Wilcox cut him short,

'My wobbly head dog was in my back window... you can't buy them anymore... worth a fortune down Bristol market...'

Sir James spluttered,

'I don't give two fucks about your furry dice or wobbly dog, don't you understand, this company will be bankrupt in ten days time if we don't rectify this situation!'

He slumped down into his chair and mopped his brow as Belinda took the floor.

'Dave, Ken, we'll get them back, don't worry, but Bill I have a question for you. Where is our head accountant D'artagnan Raspberry and his manager Sammy Quinn?

Bill replied with his eyes widening as he realised the impact of what he was about to say.

'Arty's on a three week holiday and Sammy's off sick…. you don't think they'd have anything to do with this?

Tony cut in… 'Where's Raspberry gone on holiday Bill?'

'Some South Sea Island… he sent a postcard last week.'

Tony glanced at Belinda and said,

'I don't believe in coincidences Belinda… isn't your man Jim Thompson holidaying there… sorry honeymooning?'

Belinda's throat suddenly became dry,

'Noo Tony, not Jim Thompson….. surely not…?'

Bella sagely interrupted, 'Not Jim, Belinda…. but his new wife… Peggie Strumpethouse…. she works in accounts…. and she's well capable of robbing anyone blind…. even poor old Jim.'

The muttering around the room fell silent as Chiara Montague stood up.

'I may have some corresponding evidence to support… Bella's suspicions. Two weeks ago Peggie placed an order for a very expensive horse riding outfit with me. I was surprised at the time, but she said Jim had bought it for her as a going away gift…. true love and all that. Now I think differently… it cost £10,000'

Tony exploded, 'I told you earlier Belinda, we're paying these dammed people far too much!'

'No Tony,' Belinda replied coolly, 'you're missing the point, Jim knew nothing about this….. she's one of the thieves and it looks pretty obvious who the rest are!

Bill in HR gasped,

'You don't mean Arty and Sammy… ?'

'Yes,' Belinda replied, they're exactly who I mean.'

Sir James Godwin got shakily to his feet,

'I think I'd better introduce my friend here, James Dribble, he's a forensic accountant based in Fitzrovia London and he'll take the meeting from here.'

Dribble stood up and looked sombrely around the meeting room.

'Hello,' he said flatly, 'I'm sorry to meet you all in these circumstances, but I can assure you we will get through this, though it might take longer than we would all like.'

Chiara Montague jumped to her feet, 'Fitzrovia… nice central address… I can put all my entire services at your disposal… now if you'd like?'

Belinda stoop up, 'Thank you Chiara I'm sure Mr Dribble will utilise you, as all the rest of us, in his good time. However I would like to invite him to our dinner tonight at the Pentra…. if nothing else he can meet us all in more pleasant surroundings.'

The Knights all clapped.

Belinda continued, 'Now as you all know we have two new initiates to COCK waiting outside, so Monty, Houseman of the Keys, remove Mr Dribble and Patrick O'Hamlin, bring them in. Let's get the initiation ceremony underway…'

Mr Dribble Blinked;

Chapter 4;

Initiation;

Patrick O'Hamlin led a blindfolded Natasha Biles and Samantha Jones into the silent meeting room. Des Martin adjusted the lighting to leave a solitary spotlight shining on the small raised area behind Sir James where the initiates were positioned..

'Strip!' Belinda commanded them.

Natasha balked, she didn't do striptease in public, but when she heard her assistant Samantha unzipping and grunting sexy noises as she pulled off her thigh long boots, she shoved her remaining few morals up her nostrils and got on with it.

Samantha Jones was something else. With body piercings to die for and tats that were so evocative Des Martin thought he'd died and was already in heaven. His jaw dropped and his tongue lolled. Ken Dewsbury however had already removed the army belt he'd picked up as a souvenir in a back street Leeds pawn shop. He'd always been a man of action and his nose told him there was going to be some very soon. As Samantha continued to strip, her fetish with ear rings placed in all possible places she could place one, became more and more obvious. There were two on each nipple, three on each vaginal lid and no doubt more hidden in places the RSM's were dying to explore.

Des Martin whispered to Chiara Montague,

'How does she ever get through any airport security?'

Chiara Blinked;

Natasha however hadn't changed much physically from her last outing with Belinda and her sales team... perhaps a few ounces of fat in all the right places. Her succulent breasts hung deliciously from her body and her dark red and amber nipples kept enlarging as she started to relax and even enjoy the gasps of pleasure she was giving the COCKs. Unfortunately in her blindfolded state she was unable to see that the suppressed googling was for Samantha and not herself. As she pulled her leather mini skirt down to reveal her thongless bottom Natasha let out a small scream of ectascy... Yes it had been that long since she'd had a chance to release herself and to be honest Belinda felt quite embarrassed for her.

Unabated, Belinda continued,

'Thank you initiates, once you are both ready please squat on the floor, legs as far apart as possible. Ms Montague, please step forward with the "Pot of Skulls"'

Chiara got up from her seat and removed her jacket and blouse. Her delicately configured black lace bra strained to contain her buxom breasts as she bent down to unzip her skirt and let it fall to the floor. Des Martin placed it beside her other clothes and quickly admired the flimsy silken thong covering her sexual attributes. From a shiny steel square box Chiara took something metal in the shape of a half skull and filled it with a noxious potion from a metallic flask. The liquid gurgled and frothed when it made contact with the skull and the oxygen in the room and soon a strange vapour started to rise from its scummy surface.

'Bring it here.' Belinda commanded in a strange tone as if she was already under the skulls malevolent influence.

Chiara had now become as if in a trance and stepped delicately in her six inch heels around the room heading towards Belinda. In the meantime everyone in the room had stared to shed their clothing. Belinda had no underwear on so she was the first to reach nudity. The RSM's looked adoringly at her premium body parts as if they were up for sale in a butcher's shop. Sir James was the first male to get his kit off, though surprisingly, he was closely followed by Bill in HR. Their peni rose to attention as the smell of the "Pot of Skulls" contents wafted throughout the meeting room. Monty, Housemaster of the Keys shuffled behind Chiara with two cardboard straws clutched in his old, but manly hands and Belinda thought,

'Nice to see one accountant has remained loyal.'

She smiled at him expressing her deepest gratitude. Monty flickered his salty coloured eyebrows in acknowledgement. The ethereal procession stopped in front of the two naked initiates. Belinda stepped forward and removed Chiara's bra and thong, it was a bit clumsy as she was still holding the "Pot of Skulls". Chiara whispered to Belinda,

'We need to rehearse this if it's going to become a regular thing...' Belinda stuffed her tongue into Chiara's mouth and sucked her womanly frothiness until she stopped talking.

Monty Blinked;

Natasha and Samantha remained squatted, proudly showing off their cliteroae and in Samantha's case, the rings attached. Monty offered them a straw each... it proved difficult as they were still blindfolded, but they eventually got the idea. Monty motioned Belinda to his ear and whispered,

'We need to rehearse this if it's going to become a regular thing...' Belinda nodded slightly and turned around to face the Confidential Order of Cookware Knights.

'Knights, do you approve of the entrance of these two human beings to our order?'

The response was immediate and the meeting room filled with the sounds of cats mewing and tigers growling. It was a sexual, guttural response from every member, but to Belinda it was a resounding,

'YES!'

By now the two sexually excited initiates had started to exude very personal liquids which had started to drip onto the polished concrete floor.

'Initiates, suck your straws.'

Calmly and professionally Chiara and Monty guided the two straws into the vaporous "Pot of Skulls" and the two initiates sucked up the contents greedily.

The sound of clanking metallic gourds drowned out the noise of the desperately sucking straws as each COCK member was offered their own drink. Maeve carefully served everyone, making sure to not splash her breasts. To do so would have been certain sexual frenzy. Whilst the potion was powerful its ramifications had been very carefully explained to the members by it's provider, Dr. Marco Ouriques. He had emphasised many times that mankind did not taste and drink the secrets of the Amazon lightly.

Belinda slowly took the empty skull from Monty and let Chiara replace it into the steel box.

Holding up her own gourd Belinda shouted,

'COCK forever!!! COCK forever....!

The Knights all downed the potion and joined in making the room reverberate with the chanting. Natasha and Samantha had their blindfolds removed by Monty and instructed to lie down flat on the cold concrete floor. No sacrifice was going to be too much in their future lives as a COCK member. This little hardship was but a taste of things to come. But the two new members had understood this from the very start and to be here with this particular group of people was an unstated promise of riches to come.

After a few minutes Belinda held her hands up again and as silence descended everyone could notice the Duchess leaning forward and taking an extraordinarily detailed interest in Natasha's glowing breasts. Her nipples had become like traffic signals and the message they were sending was "Go Go Go!!"

The Duchess Blinked;

In the meantime Monty had been super busy and had placed a large silver sword onto the meeting table. As the COCKs all leaned over he gave it a twist and the diamond cladded hilt spun around and around, shimmering in its galactic speed. Sparks flashed from its delicate steel blade as the weapon slowly slowed to a stop. Everyone looked in the direction of the hilt which was now smoking from the friction it had encountered from the table surface. One COCK member looked up with glee in their eyes, Bella Ridley had been chosen by the mysterious force to take part in the final stage of the initiation ceremony.

Bella looked up at Belinda and gasped,

'Belinda... I just knew it was going to be my day from the moment I parked my "now reclaimed" car at the offices this morning. I could feel it was an extra special breeze that curled around my totally sexy body as I sauntered across the carpark... and I felt lucky.... and Belinda, now this.... this... honour... never mind a drinking session with you and the Glee Team after our blow out meal tonight!'

Shut up Bella,' Belinda hissed, 'why, I've never seen you gas along for so little to say.'

Monty had spun the talisman sword again and once more the eyes of the COCKS were entranced by its beauty, yet cruelty, because that was what the life of a COCK was.

Again the sparks flew and the hilt stopped, but this time it was the pointed sword tip which identified the second and final participant. Patrick O'Hamlin's eyes gleamed with desire as he stood up, silent as the grave, to accept his designated role issued to him by the true Norse Gods.

An eyrie silence fell as the two chosen totally naked COCKS walked forward to where Natasha and Samantha lay strewn on the cold concrete polished floor.

'Ladies first.' murmured Patrick.

'Choices, choices, choices,' replied Bella, 'you know Patrick, I can never choose between seniority and juniority... hmmmmm do I want young an juicy or mature an chewy.....'

Bella stood transfixed as Patrick O'Hamlin jumped onto Natasha shouting,

'Mature and chewy every day for me Bella!!'

Within seconds he had his bludger stuck inside Natasha's vaginal opening. Natasha squirted at the very hint of penetration generating cries of astonishment from the onlooking COCKS.

'Bravo!!'

'Hail Goddess!'

'Squirt on Oh living Queen!'

Patrick O'Hamlin meanwhile did squirt on.... determinedly.

Bella however had choices..... was it the lips, the lids or the skids...... she took a gentle moment amongst all the uproar to consider her options.....

Bella Ridley made the biggest decision of her life and went for the lids...... and not the skids, even though there was only a few inches in it.

Sucking and slurping, noseing and burping, Bella went hell for leather at Samantha's hidden rings. The strong metallic tang didn't distract her from the job in hand. She was a COCK initiator and that was her true role in life. The COCKS all cheered them on, both initiator and initiatee, and soon all four lay exhausted in a tangled heap. The COCKS redressed and took their seats whilst Monty cleaned up the floor with a mop borrowed from the Janitors cupboard.

Two new chairs were found for Samantha and Natasha who remained naked as Monty hadn't returned with their garments. The RSM's were well pleased about this arrangement and idly glanced sideways, oogling as much as they could without drawing Belinda's stony gaze.

The Duchesses video link hissed and cackled again as Belinda started to speak.

'Yes Maam,' Belinda said as she looked towards the screen.

The Duchess held up her hand, 'I've just had some breaking news from my team in Scotland... first reports say the Steeles Pots and Pans factory has just been burnt to the ground.'

Belinda turned back to the COCKs with a gasp and looked helplessly on as Sir James slipped off his chair sliding under the table distraught with impending bankruptcy.

Somewhere in an upmarket South Seas holiday resort D'artagnan Raspberry placed his cell phone on the drinks table in front of him. He pondered for a moment about his call with Sammy Quinn and his face collapsed into a wide grin. The money had been safely laundered into a well known East German banking corporation . Sammy was also on his way to pass over bank books and all the paraphernalia successful thieves needed to commit massive crimes. In the end it had been a piece of cake and with only Quinn and Strumpethouse to share with, the money would keep them all in the sunshine for the rest of their wicked lives. He knew it was a sinful thing to do, but so was selling pots and pans at exorbitant prices. Especially when you marketed them as a Tri Oxy product when they were only beefed up old original Oxy stuff. He shook his head, placed his towel on the back of his chair and dove straight into the deep blue swimming pool with hardly a splash. Yes, hardly a splash was how he operated, his nickname in the office was Mr No-one, by keeping a very low profile and getting on with his work he'd managed to commit the crime of a lifetime, perhaps two if all went well.

Peggy was burning, the sun had been exceptionally strong that day and their trip to a remote native village had taken more out of her than she'd bargained for.

'Jim darling, rub some of that cream onto my back... just in the middle... where I can't get to it.'

Jim Thompson quickly acquiesced to his new wife's demands, it was never safe to take any request from Peggy lightly and to dawdle was inviting a scathing comment. He'd never seen anyone change so much in character in such a short space of time.

'Probably on edge with being so far away from home.' he thought worriedly. He was getting a bit stir crazy himself and wondered how sales were doing back at the office.

'Peggy was probably the same,' he thought, 'with a very responsible job at the heart of the Steeles Pots and Pans accounting team he could understand her frustration.' But it wasn't something he could discuss.

'She'd just close me down,' he thought, but he couldn't really understand why she didn't want to talk about the job, after all they were both in supporting roles to senior people and Arty seemed a nice guy to work for, a bit like Belinda.

The acrid smell of black oil filled smoke and charred wooden timbers drifted across to the temporary incident room the local police had erected to combat the major incident now playing out in front of them. None of the attending officers, fire and police had ever attended a blaze of the intensity that had wrought havoc on a modern factory such as Steeles. It was uncanny, some of the old timers said it reminded them of high explosives being used in war zones. The problem was there hadn't been an explosion, just a very violent and extremely hot fire. Another problem was that there didn't seem to be any survivors, what was left of the place was deserted, it was like being on the moon or even Mars.

The fire commander shook his head, it was a mess, they might as well bulldoze the whole thing tonight, nothing would be worth saving. A niggling thought kept running through his head, what were they making inside that factory to do this?

Chapter 6

An evening out;

Belinda rang down to the switchboard where Countess Zara of Leningrad was manning the phones whilst the COCK meeting was in session.

'Countess, drop everything and come up to the meeting room, it's urgent!'

Zara sprang up the stairs like a spring chicken on heat and was there quick enough to assist Belinda and Maeve with Sir James onto their double bed.

'Vat ist going on zere?' she hissed like an oily snake that had just been woken up from a comfortable sleep. To say she was concerned was an understatement.

'Jamsey, vat ave zeeze creatures done to you?'

Belinda replied tersely, 'The factory's just burned down and the news has hit him badly.'

The Countess shrieked, 'Ahh my gawd….. I've just put some money into zit to pay for ze new machine line… aw my gawd!!! Ve're ruinzed!'

'Not so loud Countess… the staff are listening….' Belinda replied as her heart fell.

Countess Zara immediately stripped off and started to caress Sir James gently at first with her tits… and then not so gently… so roughly Belinda thought she might be finishing him off. However her desperation measures worked and the sight of her golden, sun tanned, succulent tits was enough to resuscitate his shaken body. James Godwin had been through worse in his long life, but surely he thought groggily,

'Haven't I done enough to get a nice retirement on a sunny beach with my Russian girlfriend. Perhaps not,' he thought as he remembered the death of his first wife Arabella. His mind flashed back to that day and he fainted once again.

'Awk, awk!' screamed the Countess... "He's slipping avay... I know zit... I ave seen zis trauma before!'

Sir James stirred again and asked for a drink......

Zara ran to her night case and produced a small bottle of vodka....

'Ze best in all of Russia, Calanski swears by zit.'

It was 7.30pm and the COCKs started the short walk of 2 miles to the Pentra where the Duchess had promised them a sumptuous feast. They left the offices in a straggling line reminiscent of the Bridge over the River Quai. Belinda and Bella brought up the rear closely following Natasha and Samantha.

'Belinda,' wheezed Bella after 20 yards, 'Give me a sip of that flask with the Chards in it...'

Belinda took a swig herself and passed it over.

'These bloody riding boots are great if you're on a horse Belinda... not so good on fuckin tarmac...' Bella swore a few more words and wheezed even more deeply.

'Belindaaa... there's a nice park bench over there, I'm gonna have a little sit down.'

Belinda averted her eyes from the two swaying asses just ahead of them and simply said.

'OK.'

Bella literally fell onto the bench, for the second time that afternoon the legs splayed, but regained their shape... unlike the body plonked upon it. Bella splurged and got out her cell phone.

'It's no good Belinda,' she gasped, 'I'm gonna call for a lift.'

'Bella,' Belinda replied hesitantly, 'there's no cabs working this part of London at this time of the evening... they're all having tea.'

Bella spoke into the cell,

'Yes, we're sitting on the park bench outside the offices... you know... the one you and Jimena Banks used to snog on... yeah, that's it... see you in five.'

'Who were you talking to Bella?' asked Belinda.

'Don't worry Belinda, it's my brother, Benny... didn't he tell you he's a distribution executive in the milk industry.... he's a primary worker... he can travel anywhere on business.'

Belinda Blinked;

After another four mouthfuls each of gorgeous Chards, Bella and Belinda were ready for anything... and six minutes later a milk float (small open sided truck electrically powered which delivers milk bottles in London) pulled up beside them. Benny Bella's Brother jumped out of the cab and shouted,

'Hi Sis..... well hello gorgeous, didn't expect to see you here.... want a quick fumble on the crates?'

Bella cringed and said,

'Don't be so rude to my Boss Benny… but we want to get to the Pentra as quick as possible.'

Benny smirked and said,

'Yes… it's all right when the cream is on the other side… isn't it!'

Belinda grinned, 'Yes, Benny, Bella's Brother… it is, now shove it!'

Benny gunned the milk float hard and within five minutes they were at the Pentra's entrance, just in time to greet the first of the COCKs.

Meanwhile Des Martin had collected Sir James and Countess Zara in his old van. Dressed as refuse cleansing officials in old overalls hoisted from the janitor's cupboard, they were only cursorily stopped by a team of police ensuring the area was safe from marauding criminals.

'Oh hey mate,' Des said in his matter of fact way, 'Yeah, my luck… I've got the oldies with me on this run… take a look in the back… it's all refuse… found it in that carpark over there… they should be locked up for littering.. that's all I can say.'

The coppers made Des open his sliding tailgate and mused at the amount of plastic he had in the back.

'OK matey,' the officer in charge said, 'you're good… off you go!'

Des spun the wheels, the old van coughed, spluttered and covered the cops in a cloud of thick black smoke.

Belinda and Bella, dressed in their red riding outfits stood at the Pentra's entrance with a recovering Sir James and Zara, welcoming the COCKs to the venue. Countess Zara was wearing a long rose coloured cocktail dress and had her tiara plonked on her golden curls. Meanwhile Sir James had changed into a dinner suit… which was very posh, if totally random for a man going into bankruptcy. Appearances however deceived the reality… the COCKs needed picking up… they'd had a hard day and this was all about perception… and lots of booze.

Champagne and canapes were served until the gong was gonged and they all strode as one into the dining room. Seated at the top of the long table was an undressed Duchess in all her naked glory.

'Good evening, one and all, my beloved COCKs,' she boomed as her lugubrious tits swayed dangerously close to the flickering candles on the oak table…

'Please feel free to strip off as I have and leave your worldly woes on the doorstep. This is an evening of celebration, even debauchery, amongst much sadness and of course despondency… I have only sorrow to impart, the factory is no more, but we shall rise like the phoenix, from the ashes and the new born shall conquer the earth. Amen.'

The COCKs cheered, sat down and started glugging the Chards which was freely flowing.

Bella still had her boots on…… as had Belinda, but no one noticed as they sat down besides Sir James and the Duchess.

'Pass the wine Belinda… I'm going to get pissed.' whispered Bella across the Duchess.

'Belinda dear, not too much,' whispered the Duchess, 'we have an important Vroom in 45 minutes time… the PM needs to have a word…

National Security has been compromised, backs to the wall and all that…. I'm sorry, duty calls….'

Belinda Blinked;

The aperitifs and entrees were quickly brought to the long table and the COCKs tucked in as if it was going to be their last meal. In the interval just as the plates were being cleared, Belinda had a chance to look around the dining room. There were surprisingly several other diners present and Belinda recognised quite a few of them. Her clients Greta and Hans Schweinsteiger waved briefly at her from a table in the far corner of the room. Belinda's nipples stirred at the sight of their smiling faces.

On the other side Contessa Lucia and Aldo Felini raised their hands in welcome... Belinda's mind lurched into freefall when she saw the handsome Italian oligarch give her a little hidden waggle of his fingers. Her pussy started to drool.

Penelope Pollet was dining alone in front of a coloured glass window, where the evening sunshine leant her olive skin even more sexual tonality. Belinda's heart started racing... why there were enough sexual opportunities in this room to get through another ten evenings of office tedium. If only she could borrow Benny Bella's Brother's milk float each evening, why she'd be having a bomb of a time.

The Duchess put a hand on Belinda's naked breast and tweaked her nipple until it became much harder.

'Calm down Belinda... I can see you getting wetter, I assure you, that you will achieve your deepest desires with all these wonderful people before this situation is resolved. I promise.'

Belinda smiled, deep down she knew what the Duchess had said was true, but she'd always been a devious old bird and Belinda now knew there was always a price to be paid for any favour given.

'Thank you m'Lady.' Belinda replied as she put her hand on the Duchess's upper thigh. It felt unusually cold to the touch and Belinda looked at her more closely.

Belinda gasped, the Duchess was in a cold sweat, she'd never seen her like this before, what was going on she wondered and more importantly, how did she fit into it?

The main course was served and before the Old Tawny Port was sent round, because there was no dessert dish... no doubt due to their cashflow strickened times, Natasha and Samantha stood up and took the small stage situated at the end of the Steeles Pots and Pans table.

'Good evening all,' Natasha bellowed out, 'nice to see you all looking so fit and healthy...' she pushed her fabulous tits a bit further out and gave them a little wiggle. Des Martin and Patrick O'Hamlin clapped loudly in appreciation.

'Wait for it boyos...' Natasha responded, 'We'd like to say thankyou for accepting us into the COCKhood and in return we're going to start our training duties right here, right now... Samantha...'

'Thank you Natasha...... ' Samantha wiggled her waist sexily and somewhere from deep inside her a noise like a cymbal echoed, hauntingly, eerily, like a toll bell.

'So we're going to do a little body language exercise, as sales people you'll all know a person says more from their body than from their mouth, for example...'

Samantha opened her arms wide and bent forward showing the cleavage between her breasts opening, very slowly, wider and wider. The RSM's were transfixed, with eyes on very long stalks they followed every piece of body language Samantha ever uttered.

Natasha broke the spell and nodding her head said,

'Yes... that means welcome.. and you're all very welcome... to come to our room back in the offices and discuss your innermost training desires or fears with us... no exceptions.'

The COCKs all applauded loudly and started to pass the Port.

Natasha held up her hands... 'Our training schedule starts full time tomorrow morning at 10.30 am just after breakfast, we'll see you all then.'

That said she and Samantha did a little erotic dance lasting a whole 12 minutes and sat down.

The Duchess stood up and thanked the two trainers on behalf of the Pentra adding,

'It is now time for Belinda and I to retire to my control centre and develop a strategy to get us through the next few weeks... in the meantime, enjoy the fine wines and cigars... Belinda, come with me.

Belinda and the Duchess went over to Belinda's clients on the surrounding tables and wished them well, saying they would see them later for a late night toddie. This news was well received and duty done they disappeared to the lifts. It was a quick journey up to the Duchess's penthouse suite as it was situated on the fourth and highest floor of the hotel.

'I've decided to set up shop here for the next few weeks Belinda... to be on hand in this moment of crisis for Steeles Pots and Pans... and of course for you'.

The Duchess put her icy hand on Belinda's ass and guided her to what looked like a closet door. She put her hand onto a dirty mark on the wall and the doorway opened noiselessly. Inside the low hum of high powered machinery was only disturbed by a loud snoring noise.

'Don't worry Belinda, it's only Clarence, he's had enough whiskey to sleep through the whole night... thankfully.' she added... thankfully.

Belinda Blinked;

The Duchess sat down at her massive desk and put a chiffon scarf over her tits. She threw one at Belinda and instructed her to do the same.

'I do believe in keeping work separate from one's home life. Now let me bring you up to speed. Everything you've heard this afternoon and tonight is the truth, D'artangan Raspberry and his accountancy team have certainly defrauded Steeles, but we have no idea who... or what, has burnt down the factory. What we do know is that your three competitors have also had their factory's destroyed tonight. It's starting to look like a world wide plot to corner the Pots and Pans industry. That my dear Belinda is why...' the Duchess glanced at her large fluorescent yellow watch 'we have a vroom meeting with the PM in three minutes. This has now become a matter of a national disaster... how can the British people continue their daily lives without cookware... why all of society will be starving in a matter of weeks.'

Belinda nodded her head, understanding immediately how dire their situation was; worry flooded into her furthest brain recesses. Never in her short career had she experienced such a critical situation that demanded so much action.

At that moment the video link spluttered into life and cut across her unfinished thoughts. The PM's grave face filled the screen as the Duchess pulled her chiffon scarf closer to her pulsating breasts. Belinda instinctively did the same.

'Duchess, Belinda, thank you for cutting short your dinner to join me in this conversation, I'm sorry there was no dessert course... there's a

European wide shortage of spoons already. In fact the experts... so called experts, I have to add, as this has all rather suddenly blown up in our faces, the experts have tentatively given us 69 days to get this sorted.'

Belinda Blinked;

The Duchess gasped... 'Prime Minister.... 69 days... but that's just short of ten weeks, shorter than my summer holidays in Cornwall...'

The PM held his hands up in surrender,

'I know old girl... it gets worse, we're contemplating abolishing summer completely... with a shortage of spoons already and we're only on day 1, how do we expect to eat any form of ice cream this summer? Answer me that?'

The Duchess fell silent. Belinda felt it was her time to take the lead.

'PM... surely we must have a supply stached away with perhaps the military?

'Good thinking Belinda... unfortunately, they're all plastic, no decent citizen would consider using them... no we'll just have to get a new factory up and running in let's say 10 days... and you Belinda are the one chosen by us here in Westminster to do it.'

Belinda Blinked;

'Prime Minister,' Belinda continued cautiously, 'I feel I need to disclose this fact... I have no prior knowledge of construction.... indeed, all my Lego houses fell down the moment I finished them.'

'Very professional Belinda,' the PM smiled, 'I wish all my advisors were that frank about their lack of competence... but we've made the decision... your reputation for getting things done goes before you, the Duchess here has recommended you highly and from what I've seen of you... I concur. I'm also looking forward to working with you in Westminster this very tomorrow!'

The screen went blank.

Belinda looked at the Duchess and said, 'M'Lady what have you done?'

'Belinda,' she replied tersely... 'It's not what have I done, but what you, are going to do?'

The Duchess got up, threw her chiffon scarf onto a handily placed casual chair and pulled Belinda to her. She carefully caressed Belinda's long flowing black hair and whispered...

'I shall be with you every step of the way... guiding, consulting and fucking...'

The Duchess took Belinda's face and pushed it down towards her labia, safely ensconced in its folds, Belinda started to suck for Britain.

'More darling... harder... yes more suction... wait, yes, YES... YESSSSSSS! Don't stop... you've got it just dandy....... Ohhhhhhhhhhh' and the Duchess orgasmed.

'My turn m'Lady,' Belinda spluttered as she cleared her throat of sticky phlem. She spat it onto the floor as she stood up and with a short sharp shove, stuffed the Duchess's nose into her wet vagina. The Duchess tossed her nose with gusto and unfailingly hit Belinda's clit several times in a row.

Belinda screeched with increasingly pure joy at each contact... she'd never been bludgeoned by a high society nose... indeed any nose before and it was just glorious. If this was a result of being a recipient of the MI6 training school it certainly blew the Gerramima St Frostfurst disguise induced training into a cocked hat.

The Duchess and Belinda showered quietly determined to not wake Duke Clarence out of his whiskey induced sleep. In some ways it reminded Belinda of her first ever shower with the Duchess just that short time ago…. in other ways it didn't. Circumstances had changed so much from those light headed, heavy partying days that Belinda wondered if she was even the same person. Tomorrow she would be whisked into Westminster to have her first meeting with the Prime Minister and set the ball rolling on the reconstruction of not one but three factories. It really didn't bear thinking about. But what did, was down in the dining room… Schweinstieger and Felini ass was available to her, but what would she taste first, how could she do it without causing offence.

Belinda Blinked;

Belinda grabbed Bella and together with the Duchess they invited their clients upstairs to the Bridal Suite. It was the obvious choice, lots of space, gigantic bed, dedicated room service and to die for views over a radiant London as the sun set.

'Welcome to our after dinner drinks party.' slurred Bella as she staggered around the room topping up empty glasses with the champagne bottle she'd brought up with her from downstairs.

'I hope you are all enjoying the moment, but pray tell us why of all the places in the world we find you here?'

Hans and Greta nodded in unison and replied,

'We're attending the recycling convention at the Arena and as the Pentra is so close and we adore it's food, well we've taken separate rooms in the hope of "bumping" into a couple of Steeles employees for our evening's entertainment!'

Belinda's ears pricked up, and she thought how considerate they were… she knew she wouldn't have the stamina for a threesome later, but that now didn't matter.

Aldo Felini piped up…

'We're visiting the 1940's automobile show… mostly Italian cars, which is why we're major sponsors… you must attend ladies… I promise you a wild ride!' The Contessa nodded her head vigorously and her vibrant eyes shot Belinda a series of devastating looks.

'We too have individual suites….' she added quietly.

Belinda's heart surged, how perfect, it would be a splendid arrangement… fifteen minutes of pure physical joy with each person… but wait, Penelope Pollet still hadn't spoken.

'I am zere on ze business… I am seeing your Mr Jim Thompson zis evening and who, by ze vay, iz very late… and tomorrow ve are going to Scotland to view your magnificent factory, where your pots and pans are made.'

Belinda looked at Bella who looked at the Duchess… PP hadn't heard the news, had anyone other than the COCKS? Jim Thompson was on holiday… presumably a fraudster… could this be the end of FiveCarr's fledgling relationship with Steeles Pots and Pans? It all depended on the next few moments… PP would take priority immediately, Belinda herself would ensure she was placed at the top of the line for a good old fucking.

'Ahh… PP…. Jim is detained, and we have a little problem with the factory visit…' Belinda replied.

'Replenish your drink and let me enlighten you as to what's happening, literally, as we speak.'

'Ohhh Belinda,' PP cooed, 'I am zo pleased we can have a little, how you zay... confab... on a one to one basis... with all zese lovely people ere as vell!' Penelope grabbed her glass and headed directly for the bedroom. Belinda looked around and saw everyone getting quite happily sloshed..... a tear trickled down over her left nostril, why did she have to work, why did she care so much about Steeles Pots and Pans, why, why, why.

Belinda sniffed and followed the slightly swaying PP into the bedroom. Inside PP stripped off without a moments hesitation, grabbed the already naked Belinda and crushed her garlic tasting breath into her mouth. PP was rampant and so was her tongue. Within minutes it was all over Belinda's body like a scouring brush made from high intensity wire wool. Belinda groaned in the sheer delight of it all and slowly, but delicately told PP all her problems. It was the correct ploy, PP was so absorbed with her sexual sustenance she didn't give a fig about Steeles woes, in fact she promptly offered Belinda 5 million euros as a lifeline... provided she fucked her with the Duchesses big leather dildo the following evening after dinner.

Belinda Blinked;

Chapter 9;

The Big Roller;

Bella and the Duchess had been making light work of the Schweinsteigers, and the way was clear for Belinda to entertain Aldo and the Contessa. As pieces of male and female Schweinsteiger clothing were tossed around the large room, they were quickly joined by the Contessa's leopard print jump suit and Aldo's white linen two piece. Belinda quickly scrunched her vagina up against Aldo's cock and started to tease his member unmercifully. The Contessa had gone under so to speak and taken his balls into her mouth, sucking and chewing for all she was worth. Aldo writhed in confusion as he was not enjoying any of these absurd situations. His wandering hands kept being slapped back by the two females and as his frustration grew greater so did his cock. Belinda being the expert she was, was aware of his burning desires and her timing was immaculate. Before he could ejaculate, Aldo was taken by the legs and flung onto the popup sofa. The two girls straddled him as he came uttering oaths only a fluent Italian speaker could comprehend.

A couple of hours later Belinda and the Duchess had their umpteenth final liqueur before Belinda had to make her way back to the Steeles office and her single bed.

'Belinda, tomorrow we meet the PM where we shall discuss two crimes, the defrauding of Steeles and the destruction of the UK factories.' the Duchess outlined.

Belinda interrupted the Duchess's thoughts,

'M' Lady, we've been given a lifeline of cash from Penelope Pollet... she's organising it tomorrow.'

'Is it in Euros Belinda?'

'Why yes, of course... they're a French company.'

'Hmmmm,' the Duchess murmured, 'I've never known a French company even admit they had 3 million euros, never mind give it away.... PP is not what she seems... she's probably one of the most successful female business women in the world and Steeles wouldn't be the first company she's taken on the cheap.'

Belinda was aghast, 'You mean PP would want control of the company for such a meagre sum?'

'Yes, Belinda... think of it, she has enough personal wealth to do this, I bet her French Fivecarre masters know nothing about it.... Belinda, you need a real White Knight...'

Belinda pulled her red riding jacket closer to her bosom, she'd lost her blouse and bra somewhere during the evening debauchery and had decided to walk back to the Steeles offices as she was. At least she hadn't lost her jodhpur's and riding boots she glumly thought. After a few minutes she got into the spirit of the thing and was soon striding down the streets she'd been driven down just a few hours ago in the milk float.

'Beep, beep.' A car with extremely bright headlamps pulled in behind her.

Belinda turned around preparing to scarper for it if it was the cops or thugs. She needed not have worried as she smiled in recognition of the big gleaming Rolls Royce.

'Belinda, it's me, James Dribble... can I give you a lift?'

'Oh... James...' Belinda gushed, 'how kind of you... that would be simply splendid... I've had rather a busy evening to say the least.'

'Well as your forensic accountant, I have to say, I have been watching you from a distance... and well... I'm very impressed with your breasts...'

Belinda Blinked;

Arty Raspberry ushered Sammy Quinn onto the flaming torch lit terrace where he'd organised dinner. He'd made sure they had a few minutes to discuss the nitty gritty before they were joined by Peggy. Her new husband, Jim, had been carefully plied with a stomach bug cleverly placed in a traditional island meat pie and wouldn't be joining them.

'Sammy, so good to see you... and in such rewarding circumstances!' he laughed and sat down as the waiter gave them their menus.

'Now what do you fancy?'

'I'd like a lamb double chop with sausages and onions.' Sammy replied happily.

'Ohh,' Arty shook his head, 'They might be on the kids menu... but I doubt it.' He laughed, and thought how strange he'd had to make his plan work with dickheads, but that was the way of the world.

Sammy continued to look at the menu wondering if they did a nice juicy Irish steak.

'So,' Arty continued, determined to get the business out of the way, 'You've got all the passwords and log in codes for the money?'

Sammy nodded his head, happy he'd found baby back ribs in BBQ sauce.

Peggy strolled into the hotel restaurant... it looked nicer than where she was staying, but that was always the way of it, Peggy was used to being at the bottom of the heap, no one giving her... well her just dues, whatever, it was all changing now. She went over to reception and asked for the Plantation Restaurant.

Arty and Sammy sprung to their feet as Peggy approached their table. Arty took her by the hand and kissed her generously full on the mouth. Peggy stuck her little pink tongue in between Arty's flashing white teeth and snogged him thoroughly. After two minutes of tongue thrashing, Peggy sat down and looked Sammy in the eye.

'Well, well, you little prick... so you made it to the South Sea islands... tell me, just what have you fucked up on the way?

Sammy Quinn squiggeled in his rattan bamboo seat and squeaked as best he could,

'Nathing Peggy, absolutely nathing... the whole ting went to plan just how you and Arty here said it would... I'm very happy to be with yus...'

Arty coughed and said, 'Yes, Peggy... Sammy's done his bit... we're rich!'

Peggy laughed out loud and plonked herself onto the empty chair.

James Dribble was a fast driver when he was on a promise and within a few minutes they screeched into the Steeles Pots and Pans carpark. Within seconds he and Belinda had transferred to the roomy rear seats of the leather cladded Rolls and Belinda had removed her red riding jacket. James put his hands on her magnificent tits and thanked his good luck for delivering his every desire. He fondled her nipples gently, moved his hand up and down her back, pushing further and further down so he could massage the base of Belinda's jodhpur covered spine. He knew from his time in Thailand with the company, that this was an erogenous area no lady could withstand. Indeed he'd taken a Japanese lead erogenous zone course every Friday evening for six months and had passed with flying colours on his final practical. Dribble put his learning to good use and soon Belinda was screaming for mercy. Her long black riding boots had been a bit of a challenge, but the jodhpur's were no match for his muscular strength. Soon he and Belinda were naked and rolling around in the back of the distinguished Rolls like the potential lovers he hoped they'd become. Belinda's clit was going ten to twenty and Dribble's cock was being sucked into eternity by her muscular lips. Dribble was in paradise and he knew he wouldn't be able to stop boasting to Mr Babble as his cock eventually found Belinda's cervix.

Peggy stood up, it had been a very lovely evening and her remaining task was to be fulfilled. She calmly took the silenced handgun out of her purse and waved it at her two accomplices.

'Thank you for your services gentlemen, the code, the bank accounts, the contact names all seem to be in order. She pointed the gun and squeezed the trigger, not once, but twice.

Peggy Blinked;

Peggy wiped her prints and put the gun in Arty's still warm hand. She left the restaurant quietly in a decadent mood... it was another mission fulfilled and her team was waiting outside to rendition her back to the USA... fuck the evidence of two bullets from the killer's hand. The local Cops would barely register one shot, never mind two... they didn't need evidence in this beach resort... just a medical report and some bullets... wherever they came from.

Her helicopter rendezvous was in 2 hours precisely, but before that she knew she'd have to forgo a CIA standard de brief. Agent Helga Jonker had been assigned and everyone on the team knew she was the FBI asshole of Amsterdamm.... she'd been in Europe far too long to have any sense of patriotism... but seniority in the service still meant all, besides, if her contact in London, England, hadn't been so forthcoming, the whole mission would never have taken place.

Yes... Belinda Blumenthal was one hell of a confidential informant... one her cuckold husband, Jim Thompson kept moaning on about in a terribly nice British way.

Peggy stopped for a moment to ponder over Jim.... sure he was a good fuck in the sack, but it was over, she... and he... could return to their lives... separately... him to his windowless office and her to a new assignment, hopefully under cover, in another hot sleazy den of iniquity... possibly in Northern Brazil or Venezuela... she did so love those hot Latino fraudsters.

Helga opened the door to the debrief room and ushered Peggy in.

'Kaffe?' Helga grunted.

'Yes please,' Peggy answered knowing that to say anything else in a debrief was to commit suicide. The word no, just didn't exist in CIA circles, never mind when being "debriefed" by rank pulling visiting senior FBI Agents.

Arty slowly shook his head and cleared his befuddled mind, he looked up at the star speckled sky, he knew he'd been physically wounded... but he knew he wasn't dead. He looked across to Sammy.... his blood was seeping inexorably to the bamboo covered floor... he was a gonner... Sammy was dead.

Arty knew he had seconds to disappear before the security agencies swooped into the hotel... he stumbled to his feet still wondering why Peggy hadn't finished him off with the same kill shot Sammy had been terminated with. He got into the lift and made it to his room. There he grabbed the bank info Sammy had hard copied him, slung his laptop over his neck, stuck some toilet paper over his neck wound and shimmied down the drainpipe. Fuck Peggy if she was going to get him that easily.... well he'd be ready the next time... it was such a pity he'd never feel those big tits again....

It was 30 minutes to exit time for the CIA team when the news hit that Dartangan Raspberry had survived the "hit".

'He's gone... with his laptop and paperwork... how did you... Peggy, as a senior CIA neutralizer, not succeed in terminating this piece of scum?' Helga exhaled her disgust at her fellow agent's incompetence.

'It was a darkened scenario... he moved at the right second... he was lucky... but I still hit him... to be honest it was probably a through and through... you'll find the bullet on the beach.' Peggy stalled, she'd fucked up... this case wasn't closed, there was a fugitive to capture and that would delay her from taking up her next assignment. FUCKKKKK!!!!

Helga smiled… 'Don't worry Peggy we'll do this my way from now on.'

Peggy rolled her eyes and removed her cocktail dress in one fluid movement.

'I suppose you'll need a full cavity inspection Agent Helga?'

'Yes Agent Peggy, now strip to your lids and lie back on this wooden interrogating table.'

Peggy did as she was told, there was no sense in arguing. She leisurely opened her legs wide and let her sloppy joe vagina do all the slurping. Meanwhile Helga had also stripped off and as she got to her knees, a smile glanced across her strong features, she was going to enjoy this extra bonus. Her tongue slipped into Peggy's vaginal slit and started to probe for evidence as her hands simultaneously squeezed her large tits, why had Peggy Strumpethouse only nicked D'artangan Raspberry with what was supposed to be a killer bullet. Her mind turned the problem over and over as she sucked her suspect dry. Why shoot the one and not the other, it didn't make sense and of course that was where the clue lay… it was always the same and coincidences didn't exist in good detective work.

The answer came to Agent Jonker as she teethed Peggy's clitoris harshly making her shout out deliriously in ecstasy. Stockholm Syndrome…. so common in deeply embedded agents that it all started to make sense. Helga's mind cleared itself of the multi orgasmic sensations she'd just experienced and the hallucinogenic effects of Peggy's jiz. There was no need to chase Raspberry, Peggy would do it naturally, and all Helga had to do was discretely follow Peggy. Case closed, and of course Blumenthal would be so much in her debt she could fuck her for six weeks in Amsterdam without anyone caring. Life was sooo good.

Peggy's heart slowed down as she realised she'd passed the debrief with barely a stutter. Not that Agent Jonker had anything to complain about, her red raw clit was testimony to that. She looked down at the fast disappearing South Sea Island beach where she'd spent the last two weeks on a so called vacation with her so called husband Jim Thompson. He was in for one hell of a shock when he woke up in the morning to find the local police interviewing him about her death whilst swimming off shore.... The shark was a man eater... she had no chance... not even a trace of her bikini... they were terribly sorry...

Jim thanked the local coastguard officers as they left his hotel room, shook his head and thought about getting back home to normality... he remembered something Belinda had told him...

"Life is shit... but we all move on..."

Jim sighed and went down for breakfast. He was in a state of shock. Sure he and Peggy had started off their relationship real fast, and recently he'd felt that something was just not right. Perhaps he'd been married too many times, too many dubious agreements to overlook fundamental issues that couldn't be solved without a good old argument. He picked up the menu and ordered a large traditional South Sea Island breakfast. There seemed to be some sort of flap going on in the outside restaurant with a white tent placed over a corner table overlooking the ocean. Police were coming and going, he sighed again, nothing to do with him anyways.

Jim relaxed, smiled and thought perhaps he'd stay single forever. His roaming eyes made contact with the youngish looking American, recently divorced lady, well endowed with big luscious breasts. She'd been eyeing him up for the last week... she smiled again, and Jim instantly put his thoughts of celibacy away.

Jim Blinked;

Belinda slept soundly in the extremely comfortable rear seat of the Rolls Royce. The unexpected bonus was that James Dribble didn't snore... and the fold out double bed converted from the rear seats made her think why didn't Steele's provide such workaholic accessories. The thought of Steeles Pots and Pans disrupted her joyous mood, indeed she could have called it a gleeful mood, but that again brought back painful memories of good times, albeit drunken with likeminded colleagues. At least that was how it had seemed at the time. Perhaps, she ruefully thought, Benny Bella's Brother was a good move... surely milk floats provided continuous employment?

Dribble woke up, he'd had one hell of a night's sex and what he needed now was more sex. He moulded his right hand around Belinda's pulsing vagina and let his middle fingers go to work. Belinda abandoned her deepening despair and started to want more in a very basic, down to earth sexual way. Yes.... she needed a deep fuck; today was a big day, the Duchess and Dribble would accompany her to the centre of UK power and she would meet the Prime Minister. Belinda knew she had to perform and why not now, in this luxurious Rolls with this quintessential English man. No words were spoken, Dribble turned her over, found her vagina with his steaming cock and gave Belinda all she could have wanted.

Whilst Roll Royce had planned for exotic Sultans, randy Russian Oligarks, tempestuous Latinos, they had not bargained for two highly sexual Brits and within a few minutes the central driving console was emitting various warning lights advising, "low rear tyre pressure", "full service due instantly" and most embarrassingly… "bed sheets require replacement due to soiling"

It didn't matter, like all experienced drivers James Dribble kept driving, on and on and on. Belinda was once again shrieking in sheer delight, her clit had swelled to the size of a blueberry and indeed was the same colour due to the physical attention Dribble's penis had been giving it. The crescendo was quickly reached and with an enormous blast of hot air Belinda and James collapsed in a fit of compulsive kissing. It all boded well for the days work.

Breakfast was a simple affair in the Steeles Office canteen. The early rising COCKS had been for their early morning run, showered and dressed in business attire, they were looking forward to Natasha and Samantha's sales training presentations. Belinda looked across the table at Bella.

'OK Sis… I'm off to London central with Dribble and the Duchess… I know Tony and Sir James are here… but YOU are in charge. One objective until I get back… do anything to keep the morale high… got it?'

Bella nodded and replied, 'I've got your back Boss… I'll do what it takes… even if it requires showing the odd nipple….. speaking of which… Jim Stirling flies in… tonight… on his private 747. He wants to see you, Tony and Sir James… he's got some pomegranates for us… it's code Belinda… keep the faith… we'll pull through!' Bella smiled and Belinda relaxed, it was going to be a good day!!!!!

'OK Bella,' Belinda looked at James Dribble… 'We need to pick up Jim at Heathrow… he'll never get a taxi to take him here…' Dribble nodded and made a mental note of Jim Stirling's landing time.

Belinda and James picked up the Duchess at 8.30 sharp and by 9.00am they were parked at Dribbles offices just 6 doors down from No. 10 Downing Street.

'We're thirty minutes early, so I'd like to show you the team, M'aam and Belinda.' James shot Belinda a sizzling smile and flashed his perfect white teeth at her. Belinda's vagina started to weep ever so gently whilst thinking about what his mundane pin striped suit was covering in the crotch area.

'So... here we have Mr Harry Babble... high tech expert... writes his own code to track every miscreant we encounter.... he's already tracked D'Artangan Raspberry to his hotel in the South Sea Islands... and he tells me there have been major developments in the last six hours... but he'll debrief us on that shortly.'

They walked through a couple of dusty corridors and then climbed two spiral staircases. An oldish gentleman of perhaps 75 years was sitting at a desk, dictating notes into a digital recording machine. He stopped as the panting visitors finished the steep climb to his sanctuary.

'Coffee?' he barked at them.... 'or perhaps tea M'aam?' as he recognised the Duchess.

'Geoffrey Drabble...' the Duchess beamed... 'how long has it been? Why have you not accepted any of my invitations to Ascot, Twickenham, Lords, Stamford Bridge ... I understand 'The Old Trafford bit, sooo good to see you... and in such good health!'

Drabble coughed the cough of an experienced smoker and ushered them to sit down.

'Busy, busy, busy Gertrude... you know what important work we do here, in the centre of Government... as you do yourself.'

The Duchess smiled and replied, 'Yes... and we're not getting any younger... are we Geoffrey?'

Geoffrey Drabble shook his head and sat back in his reclining office chair with a bit of inlaid silver discretely placed around its edges.

'So...' he replied, 'have our proteges met? Has our plan culminated in this historic meeting? Are we on course to save the world from all the evil which consistently attacks it each and every hour... dare I say minute?'

D'artangan Raspberry threw the wad of notes at the speedboat's owner.

'Ok... if that's your price... I'll pay it... but we leave now... no delays, and I know your diesel tanks are full... you see I've been watching you... and now we go... Kristian.'

Kristian Cristosis nodded his head, cast off the mooring lines and plotted a course for the northernmost island in the archipelago. It was a six hours trip, but for 20,000 dollars US it was the easiest money he'd ever earned. Kristian was careful, he knew easy money was bad money and this British guy, looked like bad money. As he revved up the high performance twin engines he whispered an order to his senior crewman,

'Don't let this sucker out of your sight... I've got a real bad feeling about him...'

The Duchess grimaced, 'Yes, you're right, the whole world seems to want our prosperity, way of life, even democracy... though God knows why as they don't respect it in their own countries.'

Geoffrey grinned... 'And that's why we're all here, the past and the future, coming together to make a final stand against all that's evil... God... I'm sounding like a TV executive producer.' He laughed and coughed...

'Harry, bring us up to speed on the Steeles Pots and Pans case... bring some fun into our world of doom and demoniac despondency.

Harry Babble stood up, picked up a remote console unit and pointed at a screen behind Geoffrey Drabble.

'Sammy Quinn, one of the accountancy team believed to have been involved in the Steeles embezzlement was reported shot dead by the South Sea Island police two hours ago. His fellow embezzler and no doubt killer, Mr. D'artangan Raspberry has fled the scene with all the money codes and disappeared into the proverbial thin air.... or should I say blue ocean...'

Belinda Blinked;

Chapter 12;

Belinda Bounces Back;

'Miss Blumenthal, Duchess, please take a seat.' The Prime Minister sat down heavily in a red leather armchair and puffed on his second cigar of the morning.

Belinda kept her shiny black riding boots close together making sure she was emitting the right signals for the situation. The PM was well known for his like of beautiful young women and Blumenthal was his sort of woman. Sexy, highly intelligent, street savvy, wonderful figure, nice height…. and from what he'd seen under those jodhpurs so far, a stunning ass. But that was all for hopefully another time. Today was all about saving the country.

'I won't repeat the trouble we're in, but I'm assigning you Belinda, plenary powers to rebuild the three pots and pans factories we lost last night. Here's all the paperwork and authorities you need. By the way, I'm afraid we know who it is… the East Germans have been threatening us with this sort of thing for the past three years and your old pal Herr Bisch is up to his neck in it. We're all calling it state sponsored terrorism.

Belinda Blinked;

The Roller sped it's way back to Steeles offices and as Dribble parked up Belinda and the Duchess started placing contracts for the rebuilding of the infrastructure. However, Belinda knew she'd have to have eyes and ears on the ground so she called an immediate Regional Sales Meeting. Her four RSM's were all in the office within 5 minutes having been rudely extracted from that mornings training session conducted by Natasha and Samantha. The Duchess and Belinda knew the RSM's were key to the operation, so they removed their blouses and brassieres to ensure the RSM's got their attention.

'OK chaps,' Belinda started as the Duchess absentmindedly played with her three inch long nipples, 'As you know we lost the factory last night and so did two of our major competitors. The PM thinks Bisch is up to his old tricks so I need you lot to go back to your regions and supervise the rebuilding work. Dave... there's no factory in the West, so you're with myself and the Duchess at Head Office.'

The RSM's looked at each other and as one, thought, 'Fucking lucky Dave.' The Duchess started to pull her nipples out of her breasts making them even longer, a sure sign she was enjoying the unfolding events.

Belinda gave her own engorging nipples a quick pinch to make sure they weren't lying down on the job as James Dribble entered the room.

'So Patrick... you're up in Scotland rebuilding our own factory, Ken, you're in Leeds rebuilding the Les Pueset factory and Des you're in Essex looking after the Tato Utensils works. Any problems get onto Dave here and he'll brief the Duchess. Understood?'

The RSM's all nodded their heads and disappeared off to their new areas of responsibility. Dave Wilcox stayed on and as he was now reporting directly to the Duchess, positioned himself behind her chair.

'Excuse me Ma'm,' he whispered in her left ear, 'I'll take over the kneading of your nipples leaving your hands free for vaginal masturbation any time you might need it.'

The Duchess glanced up at Dave and mouthed her eternal thanks. It was so nice to have someone male on hand who thoroughly understood a busy woman's deepest needs. Being in charge of MI6, sitting on the Jockey Club board and advising the Prime Minister on problems such as this, never mind mentoring the young Blumenthal all took their toll on her free time. To be able to delegate roles such as Wilcox had stepped into was a blessing. If he continued the way he was going she'd soon delegate the masturbation process to him as well. Dave Wilcox lost no time and skilfully started his first piece of work for his new boss and quickly found out that he was rather enjoying it... he hoped Gertrude felt the same way...

Wilcox Blinked;

It was all tiring work but by early evening everything had been completed. The only hiccup was the Duchess needing some Vaseline for her tits as Dave had been a bit over zealous on the nipple work. James Drabble had come to the rescue as he always carried a tub in the Rolls... he claimed it was excellent for lubricating his leather gear stick and steering wheel. No one really believed him, but Belinda threw back her long flowing glossy black hair and gave him a determined sexy stare which made his crotch expand for no real reason.

'Now Belinda,' the Duchess crooned as Dave gently rubbed the Vaseline into her nipples, 'I did say that if we pulled this off efficiently I would treat you to an evening of pure debauchery.' The Duchess's eyes twinkled.

Belinda asked Dave and James to leave, shut the door to her office and began to undress the few remaining clothes the Duchess was still wearing. It was becoming a bit of a thing her and the Duchess taking meetings topless and Belinda felt it was becoming thoroughly exhilarating... her clarity of thought was much enhanced. Firstly, she removed the Duchess's riding boots and lastly her sopping wet black thong... there was no rush and no fuss as Belinda's tongue got to work on a very favourite though well worn canvas. If debauchery was on the Duchess's mind, then Belinda would deliver. However as tempting as the Duchess was, she hadn't forgotten about her clients at the Pentra. Yesterday Belinda had reckoned on 15 minutes a person, but as they'd demolished the paperwork so rapidly, she recalculated the figure up to 30 minutes…. each. Her mind spun and with the intoxicating mix of sexual expectation and the tranquilising effect of the Duchess's clitoral juices she herself eventually stripped off and let the Duchess have her debauched way with her.

Dribble reversed the roller into a parking place and followed Belinda into the Pentra. He too had had a very satisfactory day. His forensic accountancy team with the help of Harry Drabble had found a back way into the stolen Steeles accountancy software. It was early days yet, but the death of Sammy Quinn might just have given them a thin sliver of hope. Like most thieves Sammy would have anticipated some form of double cross, and being an accountant as well as the Irishman he was, would have hidden a second access point from his accomplices. The fact he'd been suddenly terminated was the break Harry Drabble had jumped on as no one and certainly not Sammy, could have anticipated such a violent end to his earthly existence.

But James was also very pleased with his progress with Belinda Blumenthal… she was a real stunner physically, but also a phenomenal business woman. Today had proved that to him and this evening she had invited him to the Duchess's little debauchery party. Such invitations were rare and he was so excited at his mounting sexual prospects. He also secretly hoped he would eventually obtain a role similar to Dave Wilcox's with the Duchess. Nipple tweaking could be his new thing. He'd search for an online course the next morning. Meanwhile he had the Contessa Luccia, Greta Schweinsteiger and Belinda Blumenthal to all look forward to and equally as tempting was the question where would he start?

James Blinked;

Chapter 13;

The South Sea Islands;

The pulsating mega engines throttled into reverse as they rapidly approached the granite built harbour. It was picture book territory and D'Artangan Raspberry was glad to be on solid land once more. He had to admit to himself that he wasn't much of a sailor. But he was a brilliant thief, fraudster, conman... whatever and he had the money. Sammy Quinn however lay heavily on his mind and his murderess, even more heavily. He couldn't believe Peggy had done what she'd done. He'd cultivated her for months after he'd recruited her, and eventually had sex with her... well it was Steeles Pots and Pans after all, a company where anything remotely sexual was highly encouraged. What did old Godwin always say... it's good for morale and team building. It was also good fertile ground for fraud and it didn't take long for Arty to recruit Sammy and then Peggy.

Cristos switched off the engines.

'Mr Raspberry... your destination... '

'Thank you Cristos, I'll be seeing you.'

Raspberry jumped onto the granite quay, picked up his bags and walked casually up to the village centre. He'd find a decent hotel room for the night and then catch the inter island flight back to where he'd come from. He smiled to himself, no one would ever look for him back on the island he'd just sailed from... besides, all sailors talked, especially to the Feds and Cristos had a loose mouth. Arty smiled as he walked into the Capriana Hotel, whilst small, it had four stars quality, it was his sort of place... the female receptionist looked bribe able and money... his sort of money, could buy anything.

Francesca turned over in her bed, Arty was one of the best fucks she'd had recently and it didn't bother her that he'd insisted on going back to her place after her shift was over. Her large tits swayed as she raised one arm to switch on the overhead light. Arty was at the bedside table using her computer to make his reservation back to the island he'd just arrived from. His fake passport had worked tickety boo just as Sammy had said it would, everything was sweet.

'Come back to me darling,' Francesca cooed, 'and give me one more big fuck before you disappear out of my miserable life...' Arty smiled his big dazzling smile, the one that could turn any female into a shivering hunk of sexual desire and got back into bed. He positioned himself on top of Francesca... the way she liked it and pushed his cock into her labia. With a little bit of vertical motion he delicately caught her clit and Francesca became sexually aroused once again. He grabbed her tits and squeezed her nipples as he rocked himself in and out of her supine body time and time and time again. Francesca unfortunately hadn't had the experience she thought she'd had and soon orgasmed... once, twice, thrice... and fell deeply asleep thoroughly contented.

The evening of debauchery had started well for James Dribble, Belinda had organised him to spend 30 minutes with the French bird they called PP. After that he'd enjoyed the delicious Contessa Luccia for another 30 minutes and then the totally insatiable Greta Schweinsteiger. But then things went pear shaped... Harry Drabble had texted him about a break through in the Steeles fraud case and he had to report to the Duchess asap. The Duchess was alone when he entered her private office in the Pentra and he hoped he'd get the job of stimulating her nipples as once again she was braless.

'Sit down James.'

The sexually deranged Duchess ordered with a suggestive flick of her hand.

'We've tracked Raspberry to a little upmarket tourist island in the north of the South Sea Islands. One of our "contacts" took him there by boat this morning. I've ordered a SPLAT team to detain him... they'll be in position by midday their time. It seems to be all over.'

James Dribble wanted to reply by asking the Duchess if she needed any sort of massage.... preferably by tongue as she looked as if she could do with a little pick me up. But he sensed the timing wasn't just right, so instead he asked a very pertinent and life saving career question.

'Has Harry Drabble accessed the money yet?'

'Yes... it's all back in the Steeles bank account... they're viable again... thanks in no small way to your excellent team. Congratulations are in order... I believe Ms Blumenthal will be thanking you personally later on tonight after her hectic schedule of this evening has been completed.'

'I understand M'aam... thank you for the kind words.'

'Yes,' the Duchess replied, 'kind words, but they don't put icing on the cake do they James?'

Dribble thought about it for a moment and answered,

'To be honest my lady, I'm also a pretty good baker, I know how to do icing and I know how to bake cakes... perhaps I could show you...'

The Duchess sighed, this job would be the death of her,

'James, I was hoping you would understand... get these fucking long black riding boots off my very long horsey legs right now...'

At breakfast in the Steeles canteen, which did a far better bacon and egg sarni than the Pentra, the Duchess sat down at Dribbble and Belinda's table and said,

'Belinda, darling... I'm afraid I'm going to have to ask you a favour...'

'Why M'aam... anything... you don't need to ask... you know that... why would you ask?'

'Belinda, it means putting you through a traumatic time which I know you can handle, but it's something you don't need on your plate right now.'

Belinda squirmed, what was this bloody woman up to now... OK she was head of MI6 and all that stuff, but why couldn't she just ask the question...'

'I need to requisition Dave Wilcox... I'm sorry, I know it's a sign of weakness, I know we... in the higher echelons, and to be honest you'll soon be joining us, should be totally self fulfilling, but... Wilcox... he's sooo good at masturbation... besides, it's an order and don't you say no!'

Belinda thought for a full minute before answering. Was this an opportunity to kick against the traces, say she didn't want any part of what the Duchess was offering? No... this was an opportunity to consolidate her future and change the world to her way of thinking... a better world, one where Belinda's like her could get to the position of RSM and make a difference.

'My lady, are you giving me an opportunity to recruit a new Regional Sales Manager... someone who just might sell some pots and pans, someone who could understand the new ethos sweeping this company... this country... someone who...'

Belinda stopped and had a quick reality check... the money was back in the Steeles bank account, the factory was virtually rebuilt, everything was as it should be, and Dave Wilcox had found a job he really wanted... God, did the Duchess know she was taking on a lame duck... could he continue to say "quack, quack" every time she shook her cervix?

Belinda Blinked;

Printed in Great Britain
by Amazon

79218496R00047